DUMB SHOW

DUMB SHOW

by

Susan Hartman

A University of Central Florida Book

UNIVERSITY PRESSES OF FLORIDA
FAMU/FAU/FIU/FSU/UCF/UF/UNF/USF/UWF

Orlando

University of Central Florida
Contemporary Poetry Series

Other works in the series:

David Posner: *The Sandpipers*
Edmund Skellings: *Heart Attacks*
Edmund Skellings: *Face Value*
Malcolm Glass: *Bone Love*

Typographic design by G. Q. Nole; printed in Florida.

University Presses of Florida, the agency of the State of Florida's
university system for publication of scholarly and creative works,
operates under policies adopted by the Board of Regents. Its offices
are located at 15 Northwest 15th Street, Gainesville, Florida, 32603.

Library of Congress Cataloging in Publication Data

Hartman, Susan, 1952—
    Dumb show.

    (Contemporary poetry series)
    "A University of Central Florida book."
    I. Title. II. Series: Contemporary poetry series
(Orlando, Fla.)
PS3558.A7135D8   811'.5'4   79—440
ISBN 0-8130-0634-1

Acknowledgments

The author thanks the original publishers of many of the poems in this volume for their permission to reprint them here:

"Brownstone" is reprinted by permsssion from *Carolina Quarterly* 28 (3) (Fall 1976).

"With Cheetahs" and "The Townspeople Dream of Camels" are reprinted by permission from *Brahma*, 1978. (The latter had previously appeared in *City,* which also first published "Near the Cathedral" and "Castro Urdiales.")

"In the Generation That Laughed at Me" and "After His Death" are reprinted by permission from *Hanging Loose,* 23 (1974); they have also appeared in *The Ardis Anthology of New American Poetry* (Ann Arbor: Ardis Publishers).

"On the Ice," (originally called "Untitled"), "Wedding Signs," and "Troubles" are reprinted by permission from *Kansas Quarterly,* 6 (Summer1974), 10 (Winter 1978), and 9 (Summer 1977).

"Down These Halls" is reprinted by permission from *Forum,* 11 (1) (Spring 1973), where it was titled "There Is Always a Damn Lion."

"Old Husband" is reprinted by permission of the Eddy Dance Foundation, Inc., which published it in the summer of 1978.

The author expresses her special thanks to Walter Gaudnek for the design of this book's cover and to Roland Browne, Richard S. Grove, and Simon Taylor for their consideration and editorial help.

For My Mother and Father

CONTENTS

Brownstone,   1
Haitiana,   2
Before the Journey,   4
Near the Cathedral,   6
Night Stroll,   7
Dwindling,   8
Inside Booths,   9
The First Blond Woman I've Loved,   10
Four Shih-tzus,   11
In the Fat Man's House,   13
One Hundred-Second Street,   14
If My Grandmother Were Put Out on the Street,   15
Riverside Drive,   16
With Cheetahs,   17
The Townspeople Dream of Camels,   19
In the Night of Low Self-Esteem,   20
New England Inn,   21
High-Rise,   22
Village Woman,   23
Jeannette,   25
Castro Urdiales,   26
The Relic-Collector,   27
Toledo,   29
Nets in Pasaje de San Juan,   30
Hemingway's Cats,   31

In the County,   32
The Long-Haired Redneck,   34
Moving South,   35
Now,   36
At Night It Comes to Me,   37
Today I Walk Around,   38
After the Rapes,   39
In the Generation That Laughed at Me,   40
After His Death,   42
Le Loup,   43
During the Night,   44
Hippo,   45
On the Ice,   46
Wedding Signs,   47
Troubles,   48
Down These Halls,   49
After the Divorce,   50
During Harvest,   51
A Horse Stands,   52
Old Husband,   53

About the author, 55

Brownstone

Beneath me the slow man rises
at noon, his television fighting
like a game cock under my feet.
Across the hall from him a door opens
and the woman and child slip away
from the man who has punished them both.
Always above me, the heavy tread
of the waitress returning home.

At night she knocks at my door,
standing small in white socks.
She is tired, her skin like seaweed.
She complains
that she can not sleep, that I
keep her awake. As I move toward her
she accuses me,
at the same time gathering
me against her, into her green robe.

Haitiana

My father tells me
he has heard that the waitress
at Haitiana is going blind
from her boyfriend's beatings.

I hate him for saying this.
Over and over I see her bringing
me conch and the platter of rice and beans.
Large-boned, she stands by my shoulder
for a second, her dark eyes on my face
then disappears behind the bar.
I see the bruise
shining under her right eye.

The big fan whirring
by the jukebox blows strips of flypaper
against the blue walls.

As I eat, I look
to my right. She is staring
at me, her elbows on the bar.
A few years older than I
she has her hair pulled back from her wide face.

As our eyes meet
she straightens up,
walks into the kitchen.

A few minutes later, I see her laughing
with her boyfriend by the kitchen door.
He teases her, his shirt sticking
to his thin body in the heat.
Pushing him back she lowers
her head near his neck, whispering.

Before the Journey

On these humid nights
unable to stay in the house or leave
I stand in the room next to mine, watching
the hunchback sleep.

His body fretful,
he coughs into his pillow.
I push his warm hair back
from his forehead.

Looking into his face
I see a line of donkeys below the skin.
Their heads are lowered as they walk,
packs and jugs strapped to their sides.

As I strain to see
where they're going, the yellow-
white of his skin returns, hiding them.
He tosses onto his side
and wakes, angry.
His fist drumming the mattress,
he pleads with me to calm him.

I press his shoulders
down onto the bed, rock him
until his body lengthens
and he sleeps. All night long
as I hold him under the window,
we change places; first I begin
the journey away from him
and run back, then he begins.

Near the Cathedral

Each day as I walk streets hammered
by drills an unknown woman
follows above me,
invisible. I speak to no one,
my face set to look contained
as those around me; her presence
warms my back like the sun.
I read in the tiny park
belonging to the church—
nearby, children play on the yellow steeple
set in the ground. She rests
above the trees; nodding
she shows her pride in me. Only then
do I relax; as I read late into the afternoon
images pass through me
like those of a swimmer dreaming.

Later I sit over coffee
in a pastry shop, slow to move,
a notebook open. Through the window
I see her waiting, her face
three quarters toward me,
ready to begin flight. Drawn
by her confidence in me
I stand up, walk outside
and pick a direction.

Night Stroll

1:00 a.m. The moon rolls away from the field.
I pass four people in long coats standing there
two wolfhounds beside them
like starved horses. The wolfhounds
break away, lope
around the field, humpbacked,
their fur stripped. They cross
in a line near my shoulder
then bolt away from me, cowering.
I back away too
as though guilty; I feel that my hands
weighted by my sides have swollen in the dark.

Dwindling

Dwindling, he comes to me
and I hold him
narrower than myself.

Each week I see new bones.
I rub them
to bring him back.

Even as my hands move
over his body he is shrinking.
A child lies in my bed.

Pale skin and eyelashes,
I cradle the face of a girl.

I lift the light body,
and rocking it,
pull the sheet over us.

Inside Booths

It excites us, standing in different parts of the city
talking to each other through these black
and silver machines. Skyscrapers
of glass and steel surround us,
curtains of mirrors that reflect the clouds.
Inside separate and clear booths
our bodies glow, electric. We are invisible
to each other, your voice speaking to me over hills.

The First Blond Woman I've Loved

The first blond woman I've loved
stares at me from behind glasses
and dresses like a Catholic school girl.
She likes to be back
at her parent's house by nine
then appears mornings at my office
in black boots and a skirt
slit up the front; she brings me
porno books with white covers.

When she smiles at me, she's my angel.
One tooth on the right sticks
over her lip. She says
at thirteen she first slept
with a man, at twelve and fourteen
gave her girlfriends hickeys on their necks.

Some nights we walk the length of the park
while I wait for her to speak. She holds herself,
crossed with a shawl. I try to imagine
what she's thinking: Is she counting
her tips on a smooth restaurant counter, thinking
about her film classes or the planets? When she drops
me off at my house,
she turns toward me for a second—
accelerates the instant I leave the car.

Four Shih-tzus

The four Shih-tzus and the small woman
on the park slope: She stands
still as the dogs play, their full tails
curled over their backs.
She tags alongside them

to a bench. They take turns
jumping up beside her as she listens
to the old woman in the parka
complain, her German shepherd leashed.
Every few minutes, the small woman
looks around anxiously
counting the four dogs.

The gold one
is in heat, trotting up to big dogs.
"Fritzi," the woman calls her back,
her voice expectant, without hope.
She has never tried
to train them. They perch
around her on the bench, three generations.
Long fur covering their eyes,
their elegant coats matted
and unwashed.

They rush up to each new dog,
surround it, nosing
below the newcomer's tail,
then run off. "The pack,"
she says. She likes that.
In her apartment she sleeps in a loft
"to have a little space for myself."

When strangers approach her
she seems to call herself
back, her round face
puzzled as she listens.
She laughs, answering vaguely.
Excusing herself, she walks
slowly with her dogs
behind the tennis courts.

In the Fat Man's House

Tonight I want
to live in the fat man's house.
I want nothing but the bare walls
of his living room, the German shepherd
scratching its flanks
and the thin-cushioned couch
where the fat man likes to lie.

I won't bother him. We won't speak.
He'll drink beer or lie
on his back or stand at the stove.
I'll move and sit
nearby. Late-night
I'll enter his dark bedroom,
climb
into the grey-sheeted bed,
and facing his broad, robed back,
I'll sleep.

One Hundred-Second Street

It is too hot to eat.
On Broadway men languish by fruit stalls,
their brown arms swelling
from their blouses.

Eyebrows plucked,
half moons of rouge
on their shaved cheeks,
they link arms in this heat
and practice walking behind their hips.

Under the awnings
the mangoes, the plantains
and hairy beets lie softening.

They talk in pairs;
their palms curve around
their necks, the fingers moving
over stray curls.
Secretly, they watch
their reflections in store windows.

If My Grandmother Were Put Out on the Street

If my grandmother were put out on the street,
shopping bag in hand, she would walk the length
of the block, surveying it,
disappear for a half hour into a store
then emerge with a broken bridge table
folded under her arm.
She would set it down near a stoop,
place her bag alongside it,
then rest for a minute
nodding at young women
walking behind their children,
at old women slow-walking,
black pocketbooks hanging from their elbows.
She would bend over her shopping bag,
and wait until a group
of dark-haired teenagers
on their way somewhere had passed.
Her arms would fill with jars and packages.
She would place them on the table
and begin unwrapping
boxes of cookies stuffed with raisins and nuts,
jars of stewed prunes and peaches,
loaves of yellow cake and braided breads.
Only then, a little nervous
she would grip the sides of the table
until her first customer approached.
Then her thick brown fingers would point
to the items before her, would slice,
wrap and tie.

Riverside Drive

On Riverside Drive the wind
blocks me for minutes. As I struggle
it vaccinates me,
piercing my chest.

I imagine my father
miles from me in this wind.
Slowly he crosses a parking lot
to the car. Chin on his chest,
his shoulders are contracted.
He stands braced by the door, reaching
for his keys. The small bones of his hand
curved like a wing around his keys—
his body lighter now than mine.

With Cheetahs

Beyond the book and the dog
she appears before you
in haute couture flanked
by swans.

You panic—
that the room you've been working in
has held you captive from the street.
In your mind you follow her
down the Champs Elysées,
her small head perfect
above the dark neck.

Everything you have done
falls away; nothing
has been worthwhile.
You remember the picture of her
dancing at the Folies Bergères,
a string of bananas tied around her waist.

You follow her
through nightclubs and concert halls. Naked
in Paris under the robe of eiderdown,
in Monte Carlo strands of pearls
cover her brown body.

You take no pleasure
in what is around you.
Wherever you go
you see her approaching you—
a tall woman laughing,
the feathers of her turban
stirring above her head.

The Townspeople Dream of Camels

In Boonville, the longest barn
ever to be built stands
just off the highway.
The barn's face still covered with scaffolds,
its white roof like a frozen lake—
the townspeople stare at it from their cars,
slowing down as they talk about it.
The local merchants
and attorneys reassure their clients—
"a showplace and an aid to the economy."
No one has seen
the new barn's owner—
an Iranian, they have been told,
who lives in another state.

At night, the townspeople dream of camels
housed in the long barn,
their farms covered with mushrooms
to feed them
and of Arabs encased in cells
inside the barn, their cries rising from its floor.

During the day, the newspapers
argue about the barn
in headlines and editorials.
Pictures of it drift
across the front pages—
like a giant boat, hollow,
moving away from the land.

In the Night of Low Self-Esteem

In the night of low self-esteem,
you stand in your living room.
You take the shape of a blackbird,
fly behind the drapes.

You burst into the living room,
circling above a family seated around the fireplace.
The man gasps, "My God."
The little boy runs to get a butterfly net.
The woman is calm. She ducks
as you fly into a window,
then through a doorway to another room.
They follow you, the man
quick-walking by the walls,
the boy running to open a picture window.
You do not bang against anything but fly straight
into the yard, gaining height.
Behind you the family applauds, relieved,
marveling until you disappear.

New England Inn

Inside our room at the old inn—
small rugs, double bed and steam
heat rising from the radiator—
we see
a dying wasp on the floor
making its way toward us.
We crush it with a shoe.
Later we hear flies buzzing
a death dance on the windowsill,
five of them, turning
somersaults, then struggling on their backs.
In the late evening, a fish appears
on the rug by our bed,
small and round,
barely breathing . . .

High Rise

Scream-talking from the only high-rise
on the old Massachusetts street;
a woman's voice so high-pitched, about to cross
the barrier between what a human
and a dog can hear. No breaths
between words—her voice
like eyes that do not blink. People
look up as they pass, unsure
what they are hearing or what
they should do. As they quickly
walk past the high-rise to the street's
large New England houses, they try to shake
the high notes of wild birds
or radios from their ears.

Village Woman

The village woman recounts
deaths and the sale of houses.
Slow-talking, she tells those who have been away
of the hospitalizations
of ten year olds,
the weddings of those in their sixties.
She serves food as she talks.
She eats with her hands
and a knife.

She watches her daughter's skin
and hair for signs
of ailments, stares
between the girl's legs
as her daughter greets visitors.
One night she has a premonition
of snipers and warns her not to sit
in parked cars or wear her hair loose.

She listens to those
who come to her distraught
or trance-like, feeling that they can not walk
or do not want to.
"Stop thinking about this,"
she says, "Walk."

Her own mother
is in the hospital, her huge body

being searched for a malignacy.
The old woman, pain in her joints, sours.
She snaps at those around her,
makes lion-faces at her soup,
then cries, saying alternately
that she wants to kill herself
and that she wants to see her sweetheart.
The village woman
helps her sit up in bed,
combs her yellow-silver hair.
Her mother pulls away from her touch,
sharply says that she is "bad,"
that her cooking stinks.
As she sleeps, the village woman
watches her, puzzled;
for the first time she mourns.

Jeannette

To a young woman, looking for signs of age,
she says, "There is nothing
you can anticipate. You will
change like Jeannette.
At fifty her hair pulled high,
her cheekbones sharp, eyes like birds',
people came to her for advice.
At fifty-eight her nose
was prominent,
her face slightly bloated.
She wore a pompadour.
People thought she disapproved.
At sixty-three she frowned,
her eyes larger, her hair
drawn into buns at the back
and on each side of her head.
People were afraid of her.
At sixty-seven she laughed—
a rake—her eyes hooded,
her breasts fallen.
People began to enjoy her and listened.
At seventy-three
her forehead rose above her eyes,
her mouth relaxed, her hair cut short,
only one eye was open;
people thought her beautiful."

Castro Urdiales

In this town we walk down steps
to a grotto; water rushes
against the stone door.
A rock or a bird flies
over a wall. Two little girls
dressed as brides come toward us,
smiling into each other's shoulders.

At night by accident
we take a room in a whore house.
women scurry to the bathroom
and back. Laughter—
ice thrown against a bureau.

We walk past eyes narrowed
in cafés. Every hour
eight notes of chimes
fill the streets like gunshot.

In this town, everyone's hands
are too big or too small.
People answer slowly,
a secret pin behind their faces.

The Relic-Collector

An old woman
climbs on the train, swathed in black.
Her small body passes me,
girl's eyes in her nutshell face.
She smiles, nodding to everyone.

I sit in the corner seat
by the window. Spotting me
she leans over, her teeth
rotted like trees. Spanish
splits through them,
her small face vibrating.

I edge away from her, explain
I don't know Spanish;
angrily
she presses her face up to mine.

The woman next to her holds her back,
rolls her eyes in apology.
The old woman closes her eyes
and crosses herself.

Her eyes open again, she laughs
and calls out
to the other people on the train.

At my stop, I get up quickly. Alarmed
the old woman rises to block my path.
People help me slip by her:
the relic-collector,
clutching her small bag filled
with teeth, bits of clothing and bones.

Toledo

On Calle Linda
we see a crowd in front of a church—
a statue emerging from its doors.
It rides down the church steps
facing a line of Guardia Civil.
Carbines braced against their shoulders
they pivot on black boots
slow-marching behind the statue.
The village elders and cross-eyed children
follow them. We join
the procession; people from cafés
and doorways fill the streets.
The wooden boy in a blue robe
bobs straight-backed above the crowd.

As we step out of the hotel elevator
two men come toward us, dragging
a collapsed man between them.
He struggles, his feet pulling at the tiles.
The *patron* blocks the sight
with his body, hurries people on.
We press him about what has happened.
"An accident...one of the waiters..."
He stares at us impatiently
then smiles, mock-bowing his head
as if addressing a rich man's children.

Nets in Pasaje de San Juan

Nets are heaped along the bank
like a dress covering a woman—
maroon piles
of soft net, a blue rope
pulled around her waist.

In the sun, the woman arches her back—
a rope of beads sinks below the nets.
A boy in a sweater sculls to the landing.
From the green fishing boat,
he reaches over to pull in the nets.

As he pulls the skeins
hand over hand, the woman springs up
without clothes, her arms around his throat.
She wrestles him to the nets,
covers him with her small bones.

Hemingway's Cats

The wide, rundown street on Key West:
I walk past palm trees,
people sitting on the stoops
of small houses, TVs playing inside.
Slowing down by a brick wall

I see a stone mansion lit.
Five cats on the front path
freeze for a moment.
Well-fed, with dazzling white,
red and black coats, they stretch,
roll and clean themselves.
They ignore me,
a ghost to them behind the iron gate.
Lying on their backs,
front paws scratching the air,
they are descendants
of Hemingway's fifty cats.
They are the pets of
a dead man.

In the County

For fourteen days I am stranded
without a car in a county of pampas grass
and sand blowing from ditches.
As I walk roads
that are torn up, lined with trucks,
lizards flicker past my feet
and bugs land momentarily
around my shoulders like tiny helicopters.
I pass billboards
and a man at a desk, straight-backed,
staring from an empty gas station office.
I reach the small general store;
a sheriff's arm encircles my waist.
His voice drawls, "There's a bomb
in there's going to go off."
Three people in a semi-circle
stand nearby watching, before drifting away.

No buses, no trains cross the flat county.
Each morning I call the man
who is fixing the car. Always calm,

distant, he tells me the same thing—
that he is waiting for a part that doesn't arrive.
My voice rises, high-pitched;
I beseech him, order him to bring
my car. He listens patiently,
says he's doing the best he can,
that I must wait. Ashamed,
I agree to call back the next day.
Another week passes; the car's image begins to fade.
I become calm too. Each day
I inquire about it cordially—my voice
and his growing familiar. The thirtieth day,
the car forgotten, I wait spellbound
as he repeats what he has said before.
The next morning, as always, I call . . .

The Long-Haired Redneck

The long-haired redneck
walks around my house without pants,
takes o.j. then a beer
from my refrigerator, grabs me,
pulls me to the floor then
gets up and looks at the pictures
on my walls. He has small,
broad hands and feet; from the chin
down he's covered with dark hair.
He leans back against my couch
and talks about photography
and how to catch snakes and grow
marijuana plants. He complains
about what his girlfriend won't do for him
in bed and then laughing,
he closes his eyes and is asleep.

Moving South

One night you turn off the air-conditioner,
let lake-swamp air fill the rooms.

You don't rise to squash the two bugs
crawling across the wall.

A frog jumps
out of the dark carpet—
sits, tiny and alert, under a ledge.

You stop thinking, "I could be happy,
if only it weren't so hot."

Now

Now I want it—his long,
dry body twice my age.
Before, I looked away
when he undressed facing
me in the half-dark. His skin
was grainy, soft,
not tight to the bone.
At a table
in a coffee shop he pointed
to raised spots on
the backs of his hands and forearms.
He opened the first three buttons
of his shirt, hunched up
one shoulder to show me
a scar, shiny and pink,
in contrast to the freckled-
grey skin around it. Now
when I can't have him, I see
him sitting across from me wrapped
in his leather jacket. His blue eyes
stare at the line of my throat.
Hand covering his mouth, he slowly smokes.

At Night It Comes To Me

At night it comes to me—
I'll give him a root,
long and red, watch him chew it.

He'll look at me again.
He won't say he has to leave at 10:00
to meet a man.
He won't sit in a chair
and when asked, say
that he is tense about work,
grimacing as if his back hurt.
No. He'll hold me,
mount me onto his hips.

He'll carry me this way to the window
and we'll stand there, one body
looking out behind the curtain—
the still street below.

Today I Walk Around

Today I walk around like a fat woman
hating the day, then retreat
into my office without windows,
and split dead ends from my hair.
I get up, stumble
out into the Florida winter.
The palm trees, which made me happy
other days, now rattle around me
blanched, almost invisible. My car,
yesterday lean, now encircles me—dead,
gold, a tank on the flat road.
Today I divorce
my small dog and the lake,
the bright Lola doll,
the wineglass and light.

After the Rapes

The tenth night you listen to the police helicopter
circling above the apartment complex.
The old guard passes your window
on his rounds, slow-hunting
by the lakeside terraces
and the paths through the orange grove.

You rise from your bed, leave your apartment;
you stand, an ice figure on your patio,
pines and the water at your back.
You listen for sounds behind the screen door
then cut a long L with a razor
in the thin mesh wire.
You slip into the dark living room,
barefoot cross the carpeted floor,
Ninety-five pounds, soundless you follow
     the short hallway
to the bedroom. In your mind
you see your face staring up at you,
your small body in the bed, half-crouched.

In the Generation That Laughed at Me

Three days after their funerals, they
went down under the village, three feet below,
and they all knew where to find it.

André Schwartz-Bart,
A Woman Named Solitude

Sleeping
under the longest root
of the tree,
I waited
for a woman with my face.

The women passed by
on their way to the market.
Chattering under the branches,
they broke off monkey bread,
sucking it as they walked.

Those women knew me
before I lost face
and went underneath the ground.

When I left the village,
they dug holes
near the roots of the tree
and poured palm wine
down to me.

In the generation
that laughed at me,
the woman with my face passed
with her lover. She tripped over a stone,
and as they laughed
I rose through the roots,
slipped into her small body.

Tapping her lover's arm, I ran ahead.
He followed me laughing.
We re-entered the village.

After His Death

At night, the children come into my room
looking for their father.

Not finding him they fall on me,
load me onto their backs.

Their spines cut me through their thin clothes,
their feet drag, mourning.

As they carry me they pinch my soft legs
and poke my stomach full against their backs.

They curse me for not leaning
on a cane and for laughing
before three years have passed.

Reaching a cave they shift me
from their backs to their arms.
They cram my body
no bigger than theirs into its mouth.

They say, "No one can live in the same house
with the wife of a ghost."

Le Loup

At night, I run off with the wolf
away from my village,
the girls I grew up with.

In the forest behind the long eyes
of the wolf, I see a yellow child,
his foot hurt.
The wolf limps by my side.

I stroke him from the head
down the back, small stones under fur.
A man warms under my palm.

Cats from the village appear
in the green and black light.
Silently they sit around us, staring
at us frozen in the middle:
two children without parents.
It is not even dawn.

During the Night

After we make love
you sleep,
and I lie quietly by myself—

during the night
a girl flies from my head
like a long bird
and stands against the wall
watching me.

By the curtains
the naked girl
rests above the floor.

On the wall her silhouette turns,
her hair streaming
above the fragile shoulders
and flat chest.

The moon shines
in her thin legs.

In the morning
cool air slips up my legs.

All morning I carry
cool air
between my legs.

Hippo

The sweet blue hippo
wandered in our kitchen,
nuzzling the windowsills and plants.

I jostled him
on my way to the stove,
pushing his round body to the wall.

Soup dripped on his head
as I carried bowls to the table.
He licked the green stuff
from his nose as he trailed me.

The refrigerator door banged
his buttocks as I reached for the milk.
Our cat hissed into his face.

We forgot him;
he stood, mainly by the plants,
until one day we noticed his blue head nodding
at us from the African violets.
His face broke into a smile
that bloomed wisteria.
The flowers climbed his head and lay
like a halo above his eyes.

On the Ice

I was used to skating in the rink,
dancing across the ice on legs
like silver serpents controlled.

Through the fence the crowd
tried to follow me,
eyes leaving their heads for the ice.

I knew nothing but ice
and what my feet carved on it,
forgetting even that I wore skates,

until my feet refused to glide,
hanging like clods of fur.
I slipped and fell upon a back

heavy with bone and fat. I rolled
onto all fours and tried to raise myself,
swaying; my paws clawed the air for balance.

I lowered my body to the ice,
slid along my haunches to the rail
then climbed upright and hung on.

I moved slowly around the rink,
facing people shouting and whistling.

Laughter steamed around the ice
as I held on, dazed.

Wedding Signs

At twenty you stared
and moved in front of the store mirror
wearing the dress
you would choose for your wedding;
behind you your future husband
sat touching his mustache.
A woman rushed into the store
from the city street. She headed toward you,
began accusing you of a crime
against a woman you did not know. Well-dressed
she pressed closer, shaking her head—
as if sensing bad luck, the salesgirl
put her arm around your waist,
turned you away.

After the ceremony, a friend embraced you
then collapsed, your arms around her; you could not hear
what she was saying into your shoulder.
Later, all eyes on him, the best man paled
and could not make the toast.
All day, without knowing it, you kept searching
your mother's face
as she laughed and talked with guests, dry-eyed.

Troubles

You struggle
for thirteen months to extract
stallions from your husband's thighs.

He stumbles across the room toward you—
you back away
and hide yourself in a wall.

At night you devastate him
playing the role
of the large woman on all fours;
during the morning, your lips pressed,
you walk the halls with a tray.

One day you forget all this—
as you stare at the television, the rain stops.
A stream of light appears
in front of the screen;
you hear a whirring sound
coming through the door.
A green chariot, tiny
as an insect, flies past. Marveling
at its minute wheels
and frame, you relax
watching the light fade.